Rule Britannia Books

Presents

"RICH UPON THAMES"

A satirical observation of the affluent, successful, though sometimes reclusive species, found in their natural habitat along the fertile banks and hamlets of South West London's River Thames.

By

Jules Ede

Matador
9 Priory Business Park,
Wistow Road, Kibworth Beauchamp,
Leicestershire. LE8 0RX
Tel: 0116 279 2299
Email: books@troubador.co.uk
Web: www.troubador.co.uk/matador
Twitter: @matadorbooks

ISBN 978 1789014 044

British Library Cataloguing in Publication Data.
A catalogue record for this book is available from the British Library.

Printed and bound by CPI Group (UK) Ltd, Croydon, CR0 4YY
Typeset in Stroudley 16pt by Troubador Publishing Ltd, Leicester, UK

Matador is an imprint of Troubador Publishing Ltd

Illustrations
by
Jane Peryer

CONTENTS

PREFACE

Living for the past fourteen years in South West London's Victoriana upon Thames, and whilst exploring the hamlets and quaint riverside boroughs, stretching from Barnes to as far as Hampton Court, I have managed to identify, over recent years, several species and possibly sub-species of resident, particularly endemic to this region.

In this book I have attempted to capture the essence of these competitive and resourceful species, exploring the many facets that reflect their ability to survive and even thrive, whilst adapting to their local environment.

DEDICATION

This book is dedicated to the many residents of Rich upon Thames who are not featured in this book, who may not be wealthy, but who love, and are proud of the area in which they live, and who strive to make a positive contribution towards their dynamic and cosmopolitan communities.

NHS
The Park
Hospital
ENTRANCE
ENTRANCE
ELIT 3

SILVER LINING

Distressing news Cressida…

Grandma has just been diagnosed with a chronic congestive heart condition.

Looking on the bright side however, it'll mean she'll be entitled to one of those Blue disabled Parking badges.

I've always been envious of people lucky enough to have one.

It would be really useful though, for local shopping trips, and our occasional west-end excursions.

We might even take Grandma out for the occassional drive, now and again…

OUR 4X4

Well Tristram, it's important for us to own a 4x4 so we can consolidate our status in society, and command respect, on our road.

Our large alloy wheels and four-wheel drive help provide essential traction for us to mount the kerb stones, enabling us to drive across the pavement, and to park in the newly created space where our front garden once used to be.

I'm sure the varied wildlife, birds and butterflies who used to inhabit the front garden, will find some other garden to move to, assuming it hasn't already been paved, concreted or tarmacked over…

THE LYCLIST

I live in Victoriana upon Thames. I am a graduate with a well-paid job in central London. I am very into personal fitness, while maintaining a low carbon foot print.

I can get to my office faster than any of my colleagues who travel by rail or road.

I wear reflective sun glasses so when I arrive at work no one can recognise me in the lift, as perspiration continues to trickle down my well-toned muscular legs, causing my shoes to squelch when I walk.

I do not have much of a social life, as it takes so long to peel off my moist lycra skin suit, when I return home.

URBAN GENTRIFICATION

Although it's really nice to meet you both, Mother and Father have asked us not to spend too much time socialising with you.

They said they've spent a lot of money on our private education and do not want to risk having our consonants being corrupted nor having our vowels becoming contaminated.

I hope you'll understand...

GET FIT!
STAY FIT!
SWEAT
SMILE
REPEAT
4.80
4.325
56

FITNESS

Victoriana upon Thames has many super fit people modelling the latest skin-tight designer fitness wear, and high-tech trainers.

You can usually spot them in the early mornings, trying to pass by other pedestrians whilst trying to avoid doggy poos, and cars reversing out of their driveways.

They spend a lot of time with their friends in expensive gyms, burning up a lot of energy on complex pieces of equipment to give themselves bodies that they already possess.

GARDEN
WASTE
WOOD
NON-
RBC
ENVIROMENTAL

RECYCLING

Mummy says it's really important to recycle, to try to reduce our carbon footprint.

We now have a lot of designer waste bins that Mummy ordered online from a company in Brazil that arrived within just a few days by express air freight.

We use them enthusiastically for cardboard, plastics, glass and tin cans.

Only last week we made a special trip to our local recycling facility in our 4x4, to dispose of a bent tea spoon and a seriously chipped Royal Worcester tea cup .

The whole experience left us feeling really positive, ecologically aware, and in total harmony with our precious environment.

POLITICS

Daddy says talking about politics is sure to end in an argument... especially if people don't share his political views.

If they express different opinions he calls them left wing, radical or even extremist.

We have several extremists living on our road. One is a consultant radiologist, one is a chartered accountant, and the other is a retired vicar.

My dad thinks that women don't really understand politics, as it's just too complex for their brains to comprehend.

He says they have too many things called hormones flushing round their bodies that can lead to confusion, disorientation and occasionally, impairment of their capability to perform their usual domestic duties.

RELIGION

There are many religions one can follow in Britain: Christianity, Islam, Judaism, Hinduism and Buddhism, to name a few.

Most of the Thames valley population tend to be Christian, who attend our traditional churches for christenings, marriages and funerals, or maybe just on Christmas day.

Many parents will experience a religious awakening, approximately twelve months before their children start school.

This is when they discover their first choice school, is a Christian faith school, in whose catchment area they just happen to reside.

THE METRO
TRIATHLON
ESTONIA
2016

THE RAIL COMMUTER

I commute daily along the Thames valley to London where I have an overpaid job in the City.

I do not own a bicycle, but I do have corporate gym membership as a company perk, which I definitely am planning to use one day.

In my train carriage I sit next to the same people each day.

We do not talk to each other as we are British. Instead we prefer to read our newspapers, text, catch up with our emails, or share obscure music from ill-fitting earphones.

Some people have jobs where they are exploited and have to use their laptop to catch up with work on their journeys to and from work.

These people never smile or interact and believe that they are indispensable to their employers.

These people fail to realise they are on board the express train to an early grave.

A few commuters always seem to look as though their alarm clock failed to go off, with uncombed hair, open necked shirt, tie dangling from their jacket pocket and a hastily purchased skinny latte clenched firmly in their hand.

These commuters usually have to stand as they are always last to get onto the train.

Standing opposite them is the fitness fanatic jogger, wearing shorts and trainers 365 days of the year. Even heavy snow fails to impact on their daily training schedule.

Their rucksacks usually contain a crumple free suit, a shirt, tie, socks and shoes and hopefully a towel, as by the time they arrive at work they will certainly need another shower to enable them to attain the minimum personal hygiene standards reasonably expected by contemporary office society.

THE KITCHEN DINER

Mummy says we're going to get another extension done to give us room to create a custom designed kitchen diner.

Daddy says we don't really need one but mummy says all her friends have got one.

It's really embarrassing when she has to admit she's never owned a fully serviced island or even a peninsula, and thought that aluminium bi-folds were a type of spectacle worn by elderly gentlemen.

Pandora
fabrique
Jewelers
Coffee
Shoppe

LOCAL SHOPPING

Mummy says one of the advantages of living in Rich upon Thames is that it has an abundance of really interesting boutique shops, especially in its quaint passageways, whose owners are always so attentive and pleased to see us.

Some of the shops are so exclusive they only open for a few hours a day, while a few of the others require you to ring a door bell to gain admittance.

Mummy thinks these are owned by the wives of wealthy businessmen, who never got the opportunity to play shop when they were little girls.

PARKING

Residents of Victoriana upon Thames often experience challenges in their quest to secure a parking place for their cars.

Most parking bays require a council permit, and the spaces that are available in Pay & Display zones were designed for a Wolsey 8 or Riley Kestrel, and not the latest long wheelbase 4x4s.

Rich upon Thames appears to have quite a high percentage of young and middle-aged invalid residents, who seem to possess admirable agility that permits them to climb up to the elevated driving seats of their majestic 4x4s, or slide themselves fluidly into the almost supine, supple leather seats, of their Porsche Carreras.

THE COCKTAIL PARTY

"Giselda….. these hors d'oeuvres are positively divine."

"Thank you Camilla."

"My Tai Chi instructor gave me the recipe."

"The wild Acai berries are from Peru, the prawns are from Sardinia, and the light organic honey drizzle comes from a Trappist monastery in the Swiss Alps."

"Fortunately, I was able to obtain all the ingredients from my local Italian deli which is just a short walk away."

"I think in this day and age of keen environmental awareness it's really important to try to source one's food locally."…..

RICH PICKINGS

My parents, who are Investment Bankers, are considering adopting a foreign orphan to help alleviate their growing issues of guilt, exacerbated by yet another year of exorbitant annual bonuses.

At present, however, they can't decide on which nationality to go for.

I think they may go for an Eastern European one, as they feel it might have better growth and development potential, and provide them with a reasonable amount of interest during the long term period of their investment.

ECONOMICS

Daddy says that we are politically Conservative. We believe in a strong economy to finance the policies outlined in our manifesto to help produce a fairer and more equitable society.

People should be able to benefit from the financial rewards of a full day's work, but also have a responsibility to make a fair contribution towards the rest of society who may be less fortunate.

Daddy is a director of a dozen companies with funny sounding names and foreign addresses, in really nice places he calls havens.

Mummy says we are very lucky to have such a clever Daddy.

EXTENSIONS FOR RETENTION

Our house was originally a three bed Victorian semi, which has been grossly extended upwards, outwards and backwards into the garden, providing us with an open plan kitchen-diner with stylish central island and integral breakfast bar.

The large conservatory windows now give us a splendid view of our new Yorkstone patio, and closeboard garden fence.

Our large 4x4 now occupies the space where our walled Victorian front garden once proudly stood.

No one objected to our extensions as our house now matches all of our neighbours. Coincidentally, our nearest school has a five-star Ofsted rating.

WHAT DOES DADDY DO?

Daddy works in a place called 'The City'. He leaves very early each morning to catch the train to work and returns home quite late when Jacintha and I are asleep.

I sometimes talk to him at the weekend if he's not busy on his mobile or texting.

He promised that he'll play football with me on Sunday if he has some time. Sometimes he gets my name wrong.

Mummy says Daddy works such long hours so he can afford to send us to good private schools, so that we can become confident, articulate and positive members of society, capable of appreciating both the importance of, and the value of good communication skills.

HOLIDAYS

Most summers we go abroad for our holidays.

Sometimes France, sometimes Croatia or the Greek islands.

We have a holiday cottage in Cornwall, but don't get the chance to stay there much, as it's usually rented out months in advance by the local agents.

Every spring half-term we normally go on a skiing holiday. None of us can ski very well, but it gives us the opportunity to pose for selfies in our designer ski wear, which we then post on social media.

Kellogg's
FROOT LOOPS

BREAKFAST

Before we go to school, our Eastern European nanny makes us a nutritious breakfast, with a choice of Kellogg's vitamin enhanced cereals, followed by toast and tea.

When our mother rises, she prefers to have a mixture of organic super grains that looks like hamster food, followed by Greek yoghurt and a mango and rhubarb smoothie.

Mother says it's full of free radicles to neutralise her toxins, but actually, it just makes her visit the toilet more frequently.

INFORMATION TECHNOLOGY

Mum says she'll give me her old iPhone as soon as she upgrades to the newest one. She says she really needs the latest one to get more megapixels for her selfies.

I think it's really because all her friends have one. It will also automatically upload data to her Apple laptop that she now no longer uses, since she got her iPad.

I'm certain she thinks that 'Megabites' is some kind of meal's option at McDonald's.

SARTORIAL PREFERENCE

Dad has to wear a suit and tie five days a week, so at the weekend he likes to opt for something more casual and comfortable, that perhaps might also make him look younger and trendy.

'Urban conservative' is his preferred style. A pair of expensive chinos or corduroys worn with suede loafers or leather brogues.

A soft cotton Tattersall shirt, about to celebrate it's tenth birthday. One of a set of three worn in rotation. A birthday present from his daughter, just before she entered into her Gothic phase.

A multipurpose jacket in dark blue or brown, with numerous pockets, many of which he has still to discover.

AREA UNDER
CONSTRUCTION
NO ENTRY

GPS

My dad says he's getting the latest GPS as an option on our new 4x4.

Mum says it's a good idea, as being a man, he is pre-programmed never to ask for directions.

Now he'll be able to compare the exact position of where he got lost last time to his current lost position, with the added bonus of being able to calculate the average speed and fuel consumption for both journeys.

ORGANIC OPTIONS
ORGANIC OPTIONS
ORGANIC OPTIONS
St John - Smythe
Estate Agents
MANDY

HEALTH

Many of us are fortunate to have private medical insurance. Consequentially, our local NHS hospitals tend to have quite short waiting lists and referral times.

We tend to eat healthy food, favouring fresh, organic produce, because we are intelligent, frequenting high quality food purveyors, such as Waitrose, Marks and Spencer and local delicatessens.

Our life expectancy is quite high due to the regular health checks we undergo as a requirement of the numerous life and health insurance policies that we hold.

Our stress levels are much lower than our fellow commuters, due to the shorter distances we have to travel to work.

Park Hill
House
SCHOOL
IM50 ME
SCHOOL
AQ7 50

THE SCHOOL RUN

Mum likes to drive my sister and I to school in her new BMW Mini Cooper even though our school is only 6 minutes walk away. She says she is concerned for our security, fearing we might be kidnapped or even held for ransom.

Mum is always late leaving the house as she can never find her keys. She then attempts to join the queues of other cars.

When we arrive at school, mum always complains there is nowhere for her to park with so many other parent's cars there.

She then stops on the zig-zag lines that she believes are designated drop off zones.

The journey by car takes us 20 minutes . . .

To Let
FOR
SALE

THE PROPERTY DEVELOPER

Hugo owns a Porsche, a black Range Rover and a platinum smart phone.

He likes to wear hand-made suits, pure silk ties and lives in a large detached house with electric front gates.

Even from an early age, Hugo showed signs that he was destined for some kind of career in property development.

Despite attending an expensive public school, which he refers to regularly in conversation, Hugo was never gifted academically and left school with just four GCSEs, a fake Rolex and a posh voice.

Hugo has a problem distinguishing between personal achievements and purchased acquisitions.